With love to Sharon on the day she was five,
Mama

FIRST POEMS
OF CHILDHOOD

Illustrated by TASHA TUDOR

PLATT & MUNK, *Publishers* NEW YORK

Baby

By GEORGE MacDONALD

Where did you come from, baby dear?
Out of the everywhere into the here.

Where did you get those eyes so blue?
Out of the sky as I came through.

What makes the light in them sparkle and spin?
Some of the starry spikes left in.

Where did you find that little tear?
I found it waiting when I got here.

What makes your forehead so smooth and high?
A soft hand stroked it as I went by.

What makes your cheek like a warm white rose?
I saw something better than anyone knows.

Whence that three-cornered smile of bliss?
Three angels gave me at once a kiss.

Where did you get this pearly ear?
God spoke, and it came out to hear.

Where did you get those arms and hands?
Love made itself into hooks and bands.

Feet, whence did you come, you darling things?
From the same box as the cherubs' wings.

How did they all just come to be you?
God thought about me, and so I grew.

But how did you come to us, you dear?
God thought about you, and so I am here.

The Slumber Boat

By ALICE C. D. RILEY

Baby's boat's the silver moon,
   Sailing in the sky,
Sailing o'er the sea of sleep,
   While the clouds float by.

Sail, baby, sail,
   Out upon that sea,
   Only don't forget to sail,
     Back again to me.

Baby's fishing for a dream,
  Fishing near and far,
His line a silver moonbeam is,
  His bait a silver star.

Sail, baby, sail,
  Out upon that sea,
Only don't forget to sail,
  Back again to me.

The Rock-a-by Lady

By EUGENE FIELD

The Rock-a-by Lady from Hushaby Street
　　Comes stealing; comes creeping;
The poppies they hang from her head to her feet,
And each hath a dream that is tiny and fleet—
She bringeth her poppies to you, my sweet,
　　When she findeth you sleeping!

There is one little dream of a beautiful drum—
　　"Rub-a-dub!" it goeth;
There is one little dream of a big sugarplum,
And lo! thick and fast the other dreams come
Of popguns that bang, and tin tops that hum
　　And a trumpet that bloweth!

And dollies peep out of those wee little dreams
　　With laughter and singing;
And boats go a-floating on silvery streams,
And the stars peek-a-boo with their own
　　　misty gleams,
And up, up, and up, where the Mother
　　　Moon beams,
The fairies go winging!

Would you dream all these dreams that are
　　tiny and fleet?
　　They'll come to you sleeping;
So shut the two eyes that are weary, my sweet,
For the Rock-a-by Lady from Hushaby Street,
With poppies that hang from her head to her feet,
　　Comes stealing; comes creeping.

The Star

By JANE TAYLOR

Twinkle, twinkle, little star,
How I wonder what you are,
Up above the world so high,
Like a diamond in the sky.

When the blazing sun is set,
And the grass with dew is wet,
Then you show your little light,
Twinkle, twinkle, all the night.

Then the traveler in the dark
Thanks you for your tiny spark;
He could not see which way to go
If you did not twinkle so.

In the dark blue sky you keep,
And often through my curtains peep,
For you never shut your eye
Till the sun is in the sky.

As your bright and tiny spark
Lights the traveler in the dark,
Though I know not what you are,
Twinkle, twinkle, little star.

The Moon

I see the moon,
And the moon sees me;
God bless the moon,
And God bless me.

Celtic Child's Saying

16

What Will Robin Do?

The north wind doth blow,
And we shall have snow,
And what will the robin do then,
    Poor thing?

He'll sit in the barn,
And keep himself warm,
And hide his head under his wing,
    Poor thing!

Old English Song

Who Has Seen The Wind?

By CHRISTINA G. ROSSETTI

Who has seen the wind?
    Neither I nor you:
But when the leaves hang trembling
    The wind is passing through.

Who has seen the wind?
    Neither you nor I:
But when the trees bow down their heads
    The wind is passing by.

The Months

By RICHARD B. SHERIDAN

January snowy,
February flowy,
March blowy;

April showery,
May flowery,
June bowery,

July moppy,
      August croppy,
            September poppy;

October breezy,
      November wheezy,
            December freezy.

Dairy Charm

Come, butter, come; come, butter, come.
    Peter stands at the gate
Waiting for his buttered cake;
    Come, butter, come.

Seventeenth Century

The Hayloft

By ROBERT LOUIS STEVENSON

Through all the pleasant meadow-side
   The grass grew shoulder-high,
Till the shining scythes went far and wide
   And cut it down to dry.

Those green and sweetly smelling crops
   They led in wagons home;
And they piled them here in mountain tops
   For mountaineers to roam.

Here is Mount Clear, Mount Rusty-Nail,
   Mount Eagle and Mount High;—
The mice that in these mountains dwell,
   No happier are than I!

Oh, what a joy to clamber there,
   Oh, what a place to play,
With the sweet, the dim, the dusty air,
   The happy hills of hay!

The Arrow
and The Song

By HENRY WADSWORTH LONGFELLOW

I shot an arrow into the air,
It fell to earth, I knew not where;
For, so swiftly it flew, the sight
Could not follow it in its flight.

I breathed a song into the air,
It fell to earth, I knew not where;
For who has sight so keen and strong,
That it can follow the flight of song?

Long, long afterward, in an oak
I found the arrow, still unbroke;
And the song, from beginning to end,
I found again in the heart of a friend.

Pussy Willow

By KATE L. BROWN

Pussy Willow wakened
   From her winter nap,
For the frolic spring breeze
   On her door would tap.

"It is chilly weather
   Though the sun feels good.
I will wrap up warmly,
   Wear my furry hood."

Mistress Pussy Willow
   Opened wide her door.
Never had the sunshine
   Seemed so bright before.

Never had the brooklet
   Seemed so full of cheer:
"Good morning, Pussy Willow,
   Welcome to you, dear!"

Never guest was quainter:
   Pussy came to town
In a hood of silver gray
   And a coat of brown.

Happy little children
   Cried with laugh and shout,
"Spring is coming, coming,
   Pussy Willow's out."

A Dog and a Cat Went Out Together

A dog and a cat went out together,
To see some friends just out of town;
Said the cat to the dog,
"What d'ye think of the weather?"
"I think, ma'am, the rain will come down;
But don't be alarmed, for I've an umbrella
That will shelter us both,"
  said this amiable fellow.

Mother Goose

Pussy-Cat,
Pussy-Cat

Pussy-Cat, Pussy-Cat,
   Where have you been?
I've been to London
   To visit the Queen.
Pussy-Cat, Pussy-Cat,
   What did you there?
I frightened a little mouse
   Under a chair.

           English Cat Rhyme

At the Seaside

By ROBERT LOUIS STEVENSON

When I was down beside the sea
A wooden spade they gave to me
To dig the sandy shore.
My holes were empty like a cup,
In every hole the sea came up,
Till it could come no more.

Wings

Oh that I had wings like a dove!
For then would I fly away and be at rest.
Lo, then would I wander far off,
And remain in the wilderness.

A Psalm of David

Monday's Child

Monday's child is fair of face,
Tuesday's child is full of grace,
Wednesday's child is full of woe,
Thursday's child has far to go,
Friday's child is loving and giving,
Saturday's child works hard for its living,
And a child that's born on the Sabbath day
Is fair and wise and good and gay.

The Table and the Chair

By EDWARD LEAR

Said the Table to the Chair,
"You can hardly be aware
How I suffer from the heat
And from chilblains on my feet.
If we took a little walk;
We might have a little talk;
Pray let us take the air,"
Said the Table to the Chair.

Said the Chair unto the Table,
"Now, you *know* we are not able:
How foolishly you talk,
When you know we *cannot* walk!"
Said the Table with a sigh,
"It can do no harm to try.
"I've as many legs as you:
Why can't we walk on two?"

So they both went slowly down,
And walked about the town
With a cheerful bumpy sound
As they toddled round and round;
And everybody cried,
As they hastened to their side,
"See! the Table and the Chair
Have come to take the air!"

But in going down an alley,
To a castle in a valley,
They completely lost their way,
And wandered all the day;
Till, to see them safely back,
They paid a Ducky-quack,
And a Beetle, and a Mouse
Who took them to their house.

Then they whispered to each other,
"O delightful little brother,
What a lovely walk we've taken!
Let us dine on beans and bacon."
So the Ducky and the leetle
Browny-Mousy and the Beetle
Dined, and danced upon their heads
Till they toddled to their beds.

Thanksgiving Day

By LYDIA MARIA CHILD

Over the river and through the wood,
  To grandfather's house we go;
    The horse knows the way
    To carry the sleigh
Through the white and drifted snow.

Over the river and through the wood—
  Oh, how the wind does blow!
    It stings the toes
    And bites the nose,
As over the ground we go.

Over the river and through the wood
  Trot fast, my dapple-gray!
    Spring over the ground,
    Like a hunting hound!
For this is Thanksgiving Day.

Over the river and through the wood,
  And straight to the barnyard gate.
    We seem to go
    Extremely slow,—
It is so hard to wait!

Over the river and through the wood,
  Now grandmother's cap I spy!
    Hurrah for the fun!
    Is the pudding done?
Hurrah for the pumpkin pie!

The Owl
and the
Pussy-Cat

By EDWARD LEAR

The Owl and the Pussy-cat went to sea
   In a beautiful pea-green boat:
They took some honey and plenty of money
   Wrapped up in five-pound note.
The Owl looked up to the stars above,
   And sang to a small guitar,
"O lovely Pussy, O Pussy, my love,
   What a beautiful Pussy you are,
      You are,
      You are!
   What a beautiful Pussy you are!"

Pussy said to the Owl, "You elegant fowl,
   How charmingly sweet you sing!
Oh! let us be married; too long we have tarried:
   But what shall we do for a ring?"
They sailed away for a year and a day,
   To the land where the bong-tree grows;
And there in a wood a Piggy-wig stood,
   With a ring at the end of his nose,
         His nose,
         His nose,
   With a ring at the end of his nose.

"Dear Pig, are you willing to sell for one shilling
    Your ring?" Said the Piggy, "I will."
So they took it away, and were married next day
    By the Turkey who lives on the hill.
They dined on mince and slices of quince,
    Which they ate with a runcible spoon;
And hand in hand, on the edge of the sand,
    They danced by the light of the moon,
        The moon,
        The moon,
They danced by the light of the moon.

41

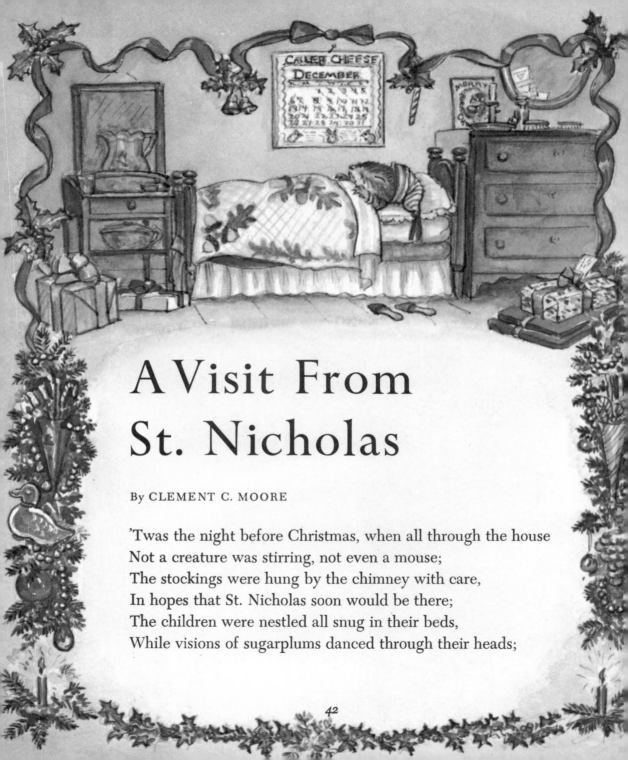

A Visit From St. Nicholas

By CLEMENT C. MOORE

'Twas the night before Christmas, when all through the house
Not a creature was stirring, not even a mouse;
The stockings were hung by the chimney with care,
In hopes that St. Nicholas soon would be there;
The children were nestled all snug in their beds,
While visions of sugarplums danced through their heads;

And Mamma in her kerchief, and I in my cap,
Had just settled our brains for a long winter's nap,
When out on the lawn there arose such a clatter,
I sprang from my bed to see what was the matter.
Away to the window I flew like a flash,
Tore open the shutters and threw up the sash.
The moon on the breast of the new-fallen snow
Gave the luster of midday to objects below,
When, what to my wondering eyes should appear,
But a miniature sleigh, and eight tiny reindeer,
With a little old driver, so lively and quick,
I knew in a moment it must be St. Nick.
More rapid than eagles his coursers they came,
And he whistled, and shouted, and called them by name:
"Now, Dasher! now, Dancer! now, Prancer! and Vixen!
On, Comet! on, Cupid! on Donder and Blitzen!
To the top of the porch! to the top of the wall!
Now dash away! dash away! dash away all!"

As dry leaves that before the wild hurricane fly,
When they meet with an obstacle, mount to the sky,
So up to the housetop the coursers they flew,
With a sleigh full of toys, and St. Nicholas too.
And then, in a twinkling, I heard on the roof
The prancing and pawing of each little hoof.
As I drew in my head, and was turning around,
Down the chimney St. Nicholas came with a bound.

He was dressed all in fur, from his head to his foot,
And his clothes were all tarnished with ashes and soot;
A bundle of toys he had flung on his back,
And he looked like a peddler just opening his pack.
His eyes how they twinkled! his dimples how merry!
His cheeks were like roses, his nose like a cherry!
His droll little mouth was drawn up like a bow,
And the beard of his chin was as white as the snow;
The stump of a pipe he held tight in his teeth,
And the smoke it encircled his head like a wreath;
He had a broad face and a little round belly
That shook, when he laughed, like a bowlful of jelly.

He was chubby and plump, a right jolly old elf,
And I laughed when I saw him, in spite of myself;
A wink of his eye and a twist of his head,
Soon gave me to know I had nothing to dread.
He spoke not a word, but went straight to his work,
And filled all the stockings; then turned with a jerk,
And laying his finger aside of his nose,
And giving a nod, up the chimney he rose;
He sprang to his sleigh, to the team gave a whistle,
And away they all flew like the down of a thistle,
But I heard him exclaim, ere he drove out of sight,
"Happy Christmas to all and to all a good night!"